Samuel Thomas Pickard

Hawthorne's First Diary

With an Account of its Discovery and Loss

Samuel Thomas Pickard

Hawthorne's First Diary
With an Account of its Discovery and Loss

ISBN/EAN: 9783337016104

Printed in Europe, USA, Canada, Australia, Japan

Cover: Foto ©Raphael Reischuk / pixelio.de

More available books at **www.hansebooks.com**

HAWTHORNE'S FIRST DIARY

With an Account of its Discovery and Loss

BY

SAMUEL T. PICKARD

AUTHOR OF THE LIFE AND LETTERS OF
JOHN GREENLEAF WHITTIER

LONDON
KEGAN PAUL, TRENCH, TRÜBNER & CO.
LIMITED
1897

The Riverside Press, Cambridge, Mass., U. S. a.
Printed by H. O. Houghton and Company.

PREFACE

A DIARY kept by Nathaniel Hawthorne during his residence at Raymond, Maine, came to light in Virginia during the late civil war, and fell into the hands of a colored man named William Symmes, who, by a curious chance, was a companion of Hawthorne in his fishing and gunning sports on the shores of Lake Sebago. Symmes said he had the book from a Maine soldier whom he found in hospital. Because of his boyish friendship for Hawthorne, he so prized the Diary that he could not be induced to part with it. After holding it several years, he sent extracts from it to a Maine newspaper, carefully avoiding, however, to furnish an address by which he or his treasure could be found. It has been ascertained that he died at Pensacola, Florida, October 28, 1871. I have no doubt the Diary was in his possession at the time of his death, and it is reasonable to suppose that it is still somewhere in existence. It is my hope that the publication of this little volume may lead to the second finding of it.

There is so much of romantic interest attaching to the story of the life of the mulatto Symmes, that I venture to tell it, in connection with his account of his youthful association with Hawthorne. The materials for this sketch have been gathered with much care from many sources. Every word of the Diary, preserved by the copying of

Symmes, is given in these pages, and I have added explanatory and confirmatory notes.

It is only fair to say that there have been serious doubts in regard to the authenticity of the notebook, caused by the at first inexplicable mystery which enveloped the conduct of the man Symmes. I believe, however, that the internal evidence of the master's hand will convince all who read these pages that they have before them a genuine work by one of the greatest of American authors. Since the death of Symmes, facts have come to light which partially explain much that was before mysterious and even suspicious.

I wish here to express my sense of obligation to Mr. Richard C. Manning, of Salem, a cousin of Hawthorne's, who has assisted me in gathering the information here given to the public. He has in his possession many of the early letters of his cousin, and from these I am permitted to copy, for comparison of style with the Diary, and also to show Hawthorne's great love for his Maine home.

S. T. P.

CONTENTS

LIST OF ILLUSTRATIONS

HAWTHORNE'S FIRST DIARY

CHAPTER I

THE HOME IN RAYMOND

A LL who have attempted to write the life of Hawthorne make little of what he himself considered a most important portion of it, viz., his residence as a boy among the lakes and woods of Maine. His biographers do not agree among themselves as to the years which he spent in whole or in part in Raymond ; they say so little of this part of his life, that few readers would realize that practically during the whole of his "teens" his home was in a little hamlet in a peculiarly isolated region, surrounded by primeval forests, and in the midst of

Isolation of his home

I

a lake country then little known to the outside world. He has himself said that he came to the shore of Lake Sebago when only eight or nine years old. He certainly had there a home — one of his homes — until he was about twenty-one. His fitting for college necessitated his coming out of this seclusion, and he prosecuted his preliminary studies for the most part in Salem, his native city. But during his vacations he came back every year to his home in the wilderness. His whole future life was so much influenced by his peculiar surroundings while a boy, that I think the story of his Maine residence deserves fuller treatment than it has as yet received. Some extracts from a diary kept by him in his boyhood, the full story of which is now for the first time told, give us a glimpse of his youthful environment which must interest all who have come under the spell of the genius displayed in his maturer work.

His father, a shipmaster, died of yel-

low fever at Surinam, when he was four *His*
years old. His mother went at once into *mother*
strict seclusion, and shunned society to
the end of her long life, more than forty
widowed years. She was therefore quite
ready to agree to the suggestion of her
brother, Robert Manning, to go into the
Maine wilderness with her little family,
a few years after the death of her husband. Nathaniel received an injury to
his foot when eight or nine years of age,
and was obliged to use crutches for a
time. He later had an illness which
compelled him to resume his crutches.
As soon as he was strong enough he was
taken to his new home. His uncle Robert, who was at that time unmarried, paid
the expenses of his education, including
his college course. He went back and
forth between Salem and Raymond, from
about 1813 to 1825, when he graduated
from Bowdoin College. The location of
this Maine college is in the same county
with Raymond.

3

In a slight autobiographical sketch prepared by Hawthorne in 1853, he has this to say of his life in Raymond : "When I was eight or nine years old, my mother, with her three children, took up her residence on the banks of the Sebago Lake, in Maine, where the family owned a large tract of land ; and here I ran quite wild, and would, I doubt not, have willingly run wild till this time, fishing all day long, or shooting with an old fowling-piece; but reading a good deal, too, on the rainy days, especially in Shakespeare and 'The Pilgrim's Progress,' and any poetry or light books within my reach. Those were delightful days ; for that part of the country was wild then, with only scattered clearings, and nine tenths of it primeval woods. . . . Having spent so much of my boyhood and youth away from my native place, I had very few acquaintances in Salem, and during the nine or ten years that I spent there, I doubt whether so much as twenty people in the

His own account of his youth

4

town were aware of my existence. . . .
I would skate all alone on Sebago Lake,
with the deep shadows of the icy hills on
either hand. When I found myself far
away from home, and weary with the ex- *Winter*
haustion of skating, I would sometimes *sport*
take refuge in a log cabin, where half
a tree would be burning on the broad
hearth. I would sit in the ample chim-
ney, and look at the stars through the
great aperture through which the flames
went roaring up. Ah, how well I recall
the summer days, also, when with my
gun I roamed at will through the woods
of Maine! How sad middle life looks to
people of erratic temperament! Everything looks beautiful in youth, for all
things are allowed to it then."

Julian Hawthorne says that his father
told him of many boyish experiences on
the great Sebago Lake; how he used to
skate there in winter, and how, one day,
he followed for a great distance, armed
with his fowling-piece, the tracks of a

5

black bear, but without being able to overtake him. He was a good deal of a sportsman, and had all the fishing and hunting he wanted.

In a letter to James T. Fields, written in 1863, Hawthorne says: "I lived in Maine like a bird in the air, so perfect was the freedom I enjoyed. But it was there I first got my cursed habits of solitude." This sentence of itself shows his own opinion of the biographical value of his boyish experience. It is the main object of this work to supply the link his biographers have missed.

The lake region A brief description of the region in which Hawthorne spent so much of his youth, and of the places he mentions in his diary, may be given here. The town of Raymond is on the northeastern shore of Lake Sebago, and sends a long, curving cape into its waters. This is known as Raymond Cape; it is four miles long, and one mile in width. Its curve incloses on its southeastern side a body of

6

water called Jordan Bay. On its north-western side is Dingley Bay with its fourteen islands, which receives the waters of Dingley Brook; this brook is only about a mile in length, and is the outlet of Thomas Pond, a little lake, perhaps a mile wide. Sebago Lake, formerly called the Great Pond, is the last and largest of a chain of navigable lakes, thirty-one miles in length. It is itself fourteen miles long and eight miles broad. There is a series of smaller lakes, several of them larger than Thomas Pond, within the area of the town of Raymond. They have been given such names as Great Rattlesnake, Little Rattlesnake, and Panther. The lofty head and rugged shoulders of Rattlesnake Mountain tower above these lakes and over wide meadows covered with a heavy growth of white oak.

The house occupied by Hawthorne's mother was near the outlet of Dingley *Dingley* Brook, and on the opposite side of the *Brook*

7

brook was the residence of her brother, Richard Manning. The store and mill often mentioned in Hawthorne's journal, from which we are to give extracts, were close at hand; a fall of fifteen feet in the brook gives a serviceable water-power at this point. The favorite fishing-place of young Hawthorne was at the head of the brook, where it flows from Thomas Pond. The large flat rock on which he sat goes by the name of "Nat's Rock." It was the view from this point to which Consul Hawthorne referred in his talk with his old playmate, Symmes, when they met on a street in Liverpool. Among the *Places* places mentioned in the diary are "Pulpit *mentioned* Rock," "The Images," "Frye's Island," *in diary* and "Muddy River." The great boulder, somewhat resembling a pulpit, is a mile from the Hawthorne house, easterly, on the road to Portland. At the southern extremity of the long narrow cape, projecting into Sebago Lake, is a picturesque promontory known as "The Images;"

8

this is five miles southerly from the little hamlet which was the home of Hawthorne's boyhood. It was on the road between these points that the Tarbox tragedy occurred, which, according to Symmes, was celebrated in verse by the young poet. Some figures painted by Indians were formerly to be seen upon the cliffs at the extremity of the cape. These were "The Images." A mass of *"The Images"* rocks rises perpendicularly to the height of about sixty feet, " then slopes upward, in jagged, broken shapes, to a still further height of thirty feet, with a few spots of greensward, where scraggy pines and stunted birches struggle for existence, seemingly out of the solid rock." The water at the foot of the cliff is eighty-five feet deep. The legend is that Captain Frye, pursued by Indians, made a desperate leap from this cliff, and swam across to Frye's Island, where he concealed himself from the Indians in the dense forest. There is a cave at the

water line of the cliff, now called Hawthorne's Cave ; a boat can sail into this
cave twenty-five feet. It is said that this
was a favorite retreat of Hawthorne's.
He mentions a visit to this cave in his
diary.

Off the end of the cape, at a point
nearly central in the lake, and visible
from all its shores, is Frye's Island, with
its thousand acres of primeval woods.
At the northwestern corner of the lake,
nearly west of Dingley Bay, is the
mouth of "Muddy River," graphically
described by Hawthorne, in his account
of the fishing expedition. Midway between Dingley Brook and Muddy River
Songo River is the outlet of the famous Songo River,
which has been celebrated in Longfel-
low's verse, and in the prose of many
noted tourists. This exceedingly crooked
river, doubling upon itself many times,
connects Sebago Lake and Brandy Pond,
and gives a peculiar zest to the navigation of these waters : —

THE IMAGES, SEBAGO LAKE

" Nowhere such a devious stream,
    Save in fancy or in dream,
    Winding slow through bush and brake,
    Links together lake and lake."

Richard Manning was the resident *His un-* proprietor and manager of the consider- *cles* able tract of land in Raymond owned by his family.   He built for himself a large, square mansion, with a hip roof, in the style that was then the fashion in his native Essex County.   It was much finer in all its appointments than any house in that region.   His brother Robert frequently visited Raymond, but kept the old home in Salem.   When their sister, Mrs. Hawthorne, lost her husband, Robert Manning assumed the care of the orphaned family.   As the widow desired seclusion, he built for her at Raymond a house as large as Richard's, and in similar style, except that it had not a hip roof. Hawthorne was eight or nine years old, as we have seen, when he first came to Maine.   It was when he was ten years old,

11

in 1814, that the house was built for his
mother. He did not live there continu-
ously, but for several months each year,
until he graduated from Bowdoin College
at the age of twenty-one. His mother
and sisters were in their country home
during most of the time when he was
pursuing his studies at Salem and Bruns-
wick. Mrs. Hawthorne had a flower garden, and a fine young orchard of apple-
trees which were kept neatly trimmed and
whitewashed. A row of butternut-trees
also ornamented the place. After her
return to Salem, the house was occupied
as a stage tavern. By the will of Richard
Manning, who died a few years later, it
was provided that a church be built in
the vicinity of his residence. His widow
married Francis Radoux, a Frenchman,
who suggested that this item of the will
might be executed by remodeling the
Hawthorne house into a church, as it was
too large a house for any family likely to
want it. This was done, but the in-

tended economy was not realized; for Radoux found that the cost of remodeling exceeded that which a new and more suitable meeting-house would have involved. The massive chimneys, which characterized all the dwellings of that period, were removed, and the floor between the two stories, leaving only the outer shell of the building hallowed by so many memories. As there was no society to take charge of the church, it was dedicated as a free meeting-house, open to clergymen of all denominations; and as "what is everybody's business is nobody's," there was no one to take care of the edifice now doubly sacred. For a time it seemed going to ruin, but now it is painted white and kept in excellent repair, both as to exterior and interior, and makes a neat and comfortable place of worship.

A gentleman who when a boy lived *A neigh-* near the Hawthornes, was a playmate of *bor's im-* Nathaniel's, and who is mentioned by *pressions* name in the diary from which extracts are to be found in another chapter, more than a quarter of a century ago gave the present writer his impressions of the family. He said : —

" Mrs. Hawthorne was a feeble woman, and withal very reserved. She was a pious woman, and a minute observer of religious festivals, fasts, feasts, and Sabbath days. She was inclined, it was thought by her neighbors, to be somewhat aristocratic. But not so with Nat. He was a pleasant, lively, fun-loving boy, and had no enemies. He did much to make their home in Maine attractive."

Mr. Richard C. Manning, of Salem, who is a son of Robert Manning, the uncle who defrayed the expenses of Hawthorne's education, has in his possession a large collection of memorials of his distinguished cousin, including many letters he wrote to his mother and sisters. From some of these, which refer to his life in Raymond, I am kindly permitted by Mr. Manning to quote. I give these specimens of his early letters for the purpose of comparison with the extracts from the diary of the same period, to be found in another chapter, as doubts have been expressed in regard to the genuineness of the diary.

On the 24th of March, 1819, he wrote from Raymond to his uncle Robert, in Salem : —

DEAR UNCLE, — I suppose you have See page 29 not heard of the death of Mr. Tarbox and his wife, who were frozen to death on Wednesday last. They were brought from the Cape on Saturday, and buried from Captain Dingley's on Sunday. The snow is going off very fast, and I don't think we shall have much more sleighing. I hope we shall not, for I am tired of winter. You ordered me to write as well as I could, but this is bad paper. I am writing with a bad pen, and am in a

15

hurry, as I am going to Portland at noon with Mr. Leach.

Your affectionate nephew,

NATHANIEL HATHORNE.

P. S.   This paper is two cents a sheet.

Homesick at Salem   On the 26th of July, 1819, he wrote from Salem to his uncle Robert in Raymond: "I know it is best for me to be up here, as I have no time to lose in getting my schooling.   Sometimes I do have very hard fits of homesickness.   I wish when you come, you would bring Ebe (his sister Elizabeth) with you, not for her sake, for I do not think she would be half so well contented here as in Raymond; but for mine, for I have nobody to talk to but . . . and it seems lonesome here.   There is a pot of excellent guava jelly now in the house, and one of preserved limes, and I am afraid they will mould if you do not come; for it's esteemed sacrilege by grandmother to eat any of them now, because she is keeping

16

them against somebody is sick, and I
suppose she would be very much disap-
pointed if everybody was to continue
well, and they were to spoil. We have
some oranges, too, which Isaac Burnham
gave grandmother, which are rotting as
fast as possible, and we stand a very fair
chance of not having any good of them,
because we have to eat the bad ones first,
as the good ones are to be kept till they
are spoiled also."

In May, 1820, his uncle Robert was
again in Raymond, and Nathaniel, fearing he would get out his gun and use it,
cautions him, "It has a very large charge
in it, and I guess it will kick."

Again writing from Salem, under date *Early let-*
of June 19, 1821, he tells his mother how *ters*
much he wishes to see her, but adds : —

"I hope, dear mother, that you will
not be tempted by my entreaties to return to Salem to live. You can never
have so much comfort here as you now
enjoy. You are now undisputed mistress

17

of your own house . . . If you remove to
Salem, I shall have no mother to return
to during the college vacations, and the
expense will be too great for me to come
to Salem. (This was written a few weeks
before his college life began.) If you remain at Raymond, think how delightfully
the time will pass, with all your children
round you, shut out from the world, and
nothing to disturb us. It will be a second Garden of Eden.

> " ' Lo, what an entertaining sight
> Are kindred who agree.'

Elizabeth is as anxious for you to stay as
myself. She says she is contented to remain here for a short time, but greatly
prefers Raymond as a permanent place
of residence. The reason for my saying
so much on this subject is that Mrs. Dike
and Miss Manning (an older sister of his
mother) are very earnest for you to return to Salem, and I am afraid they will
commission uncle Robert to persuade
you to it. But, mother, if you wish to

live in peace, I conjure you not to consent to it. Grandmother, I think, is rather in favor of your staying."

In March, 1820, he wrote to his sister *His love* Louisa from Salem : " Oh, that I had the *for Ray-* wings of a dove, that I might fly hence *mond* and be at rest ! How often do I long for my gun, and wish that I could again savageize with you. But I shall never again run wild in Raymond, and I shall never be so happy as when I did. I hope mother will upon no account think of returning to Salem."

In July of the same year, he wrote to his mother in Raymond : " I should like to come down with Mr. Manning to see you, but I suppose it is in vain to wish it."

In August, 1821, he wrote : "There are few people of so much constancy as myself. I have preferred and still prefer Raymond to Salem, through every change of fortune."

The following incident of his college

College life life is so characteristic of the boy Hawthorne, that it is worth relating here. I find it in the letters preserved by Richard Manning. In 1822, near the close of his Freshman year, he was once found to be breaking the rules of the college by playing cards with some of his classmates, but not for money. He was fined fifty cents by the faculty, and President Allen wrote to Mrs. Hawthorne, asking her to "coöperate with us in the attempt to induce your son faithfully to observe the laws of the institution." He suggested that her son was less to blame than the person he played with ; he had been tempted by his associate to break the rules. In a letter to his sister, written at this time, Hawthorne gives his version of the affair, and is indignant over the intimation that he had yielded to temptation. He evidently wished to bear all the blame that belonged to him, and not to figure as a lamb led astray, especially when so near the glorious estate of a Sophomore. He says : "I am full as willing to play as the person he suspects of having enticed me ; and would have been influenced by no one. I have a great mind to commence playing again, merely to show them that I scorn to be seduced by another into anything wrong." His college record indicates that his delinquencies were not at all serious, and merely show that he took life jovially and carelessly. In October of the same year, he wrote : "The laws of the college are not too strict, and I do not have to study as hard as I did in Salem."

CHAPTER II

THE STORY OF WILLIAM SYMMES

NEARLY thirty years ago there came into my hands certain extracts from what purported to be a diary kept by Hawthorne, written when he was a lad in his teens. In spite of many circumstances which at the time seemed suspicious, the internal evidence of genuineness was so great, that these extracts were printed in a paper with which I was connected at Portland. There was at first what appeared to be unnecessary mystery about the personality of the correspondent who forwarded the notes. His letters came at long intervals, were *First hint* signed only by the initials "W. S.," and *of diary* were postmarked at Alexandria, Virginia. Efforts to communicate with him

22

by letter proved unavailing, and I could only reach him by personal notes in my paper. He never received nor asked for money, nor replied to offers of compensation. In the last letter I received from him, in the summer of 1871, he said he was soon coming to Maine, and would bring the old diary with him. In November of that year came intelligence of his death, and no more was ever heard of the notebook, though some extracts, found copied among his papers left at Alexandria, came to hand nearly two years afterward. Gradually some explanations of the mystery came to light, and confirmations of his story multiplied, until no reasonable doubt existed that we had before us the first indications Hawthorne ever gave of the genius which now irradiates our literature, and that they came to us from a playmate of his youth, into whose hands the diary had come in a romantic way.

Our correspondent's name proved to

be William Symmes; his story is in it-self full of interest, and from it can be gathered some of the reasons why there was so much that seemed mysterious in the matter of the diary. We did not know until after his death that he was a mulatto; ignorance of this fact naturally tangled the clues by which we were searching for him in Virginia. This is a brief statement of the leading incidents *Son of a* of his life: He was born in Portland, *noted* Maine, in 1805, and was the natural son *lawyer* of a leading member of the Massachu-setts bar of that day, who gave him his own name. Upon the death of his father, the son, then two years old, was sent into the country, and was brought up as the foster son of Captain Jonathan Britton, of Otisfield, Maine, with whom he lived until twenty years of age. It was during these years that Nathaniel Hawthorne, who was one year older than Symmes, came to live in Raymond, an adjoining town.

Richard Manning was a gentleman of culture and refined tastes, somewhat aristocratic in his bearing, and found few associates in the sparsely settled region, which to this day is scarcely more populous than at the beginning of this century. Britton was an unpolished and eccentric man, of much native ability, and *Captain* *Britton* became a frequent visitor at Manning's. His mulatto foster son sometimes accompanied him, and there he met young Hawthorne, became his companion in gunning and fishing expeditions, and a lasting friendship existed between them. The district school was open to the young mulatto, and he availed himself of its advantages. His letters, which we give precisely as he wrote them, show how far he was from being illiterate. But I do not think he could have known of his paternal ancestry, for he spelled his name " Sims." At the age of twenty he went to sea as a common sailor, and we shall see how in the streets of Liverpool he was once cordially greeted by Consul Hawthorne. During our civil war he was a member of Colonel Baker's secret detective force. He died at Pensacola, Florida, October 28, 1871. Some further information in regard to him may be found in a postscript at the close of this volume.

We will let him give his own account of the manner in which he came into possession of the early diary of his old playmate. In 1870 an article was going the rounds of the newspapers to the effect that no one was then living at Raymond who remembered the boy Hawthorne. The paper with which I was connected, the "Portland Transcript," having published this article, we soon received a letter from Alexandria, Virginia, signed "W. S.," which is so full of interesting reminiscence of that part of Hawthorne's life of which his biographers have made little account, that no excuse is needed for giving a liberal ex-

tract from it in this place. After men-
tioning several reasons why the elderly
people of Raymond did not remember
Hawthorne, he says : —

"Another reason is, that these people *Letter*
do not recognize the name when they *from*
hear it spoken or see it on paper. The *Symmes*
universal pronunciation of the name in
Raymond was Hathorne — the first syl-
lable exactly as the word 'hearth' was
pronounced at that time. I remember
meeting in 1852, in Portland, Mr. Jacob
Watkins, who lived within cannon-shot
of the Richard Manning place, and knew
the lad Hawthorne very well; I said to
him, 'Nat Hawthorne is becoming famous.' He seemed puzzled, and said
inquiringly, 'Nat who?' I answered,
'That boy who used to live in your meeting-house with his mother, and fish out
on that great flat rock at the outlet of
Thomas Pond, and sit gazing for hours
at a time across at your field and brick-
yard.' 'Oh yes,' said the old gentleman,

'you mean Nat Hathorne,' sounding the 'a' as in bath. 'What of him?' I told him that 'Nat' was becoming popular as a writer. The good old man said he had seen the name of a Mr. Hawthorne in the papers, but never suspected it was the name of young 'Nat Hathorne.' I lived with one of the few men who visited Richard Manning, and used to go there often with my foster father. Nat Hawthorne and I were nearly of the same *Thomas* age and often played together. Thomas *Pond* Pond, a beautiful sheet of water, lay about a half a mile to the eastward of his mother's house, the outlet of which is the creek running between Manning's house and that of his sister. We used to go to the pond, and on a large flat rock, partly covered with water, fish for perch and minnows, and try our skill at throwing stones as far as we could into the pond. At that time there was a charming knoll, a few rods from the outlet, entirely clear of underbrush and completely surrounded by a growth of handsome trees. Nat told me that his uncle Richard said the knoll was an Indian burying-ground. There were ridges having an artificial appearance, that he insisted were Indian graves. On one of *Indian* our excursions to the pond he read to *graves* me some verses that he had written, the subject being the freezing to death of a Mr. Tarbox and wife, in a terrible storm. This happened in their immediate neighborhood. One of the little orphans, Elizabeth Tarbox, was adopted by Mrs. Richard Manning, and was treated with particular tenderness by little Nat. He also read to me some poetry of his upon another sad event, that happened at about that time, the drowning of the wife and infant of Mr. Nathaniel Knight.[1] In

[1] In Griffith's *Poets of Maine*, p. 106, is given a ballad describing the Knight tragedy, and it is suggested that these were the verses written by Hawthorne and recited to Symmes. But it has been found that this was not the case ; they were the effusion of a local ballad-monger named Daniel Shaw.

29

crossing the bridge at Horsebeef Falls on the Presumpscot River, between Gorham and Windham, Mr. Knight's horse became unmanageable and backed the sleigh off the bridge, and Mrs. Knight was thrown from a great height, struck the water, and was carried under the ice below the falls. I cannot recall a single line of his poetry, but remember that he read with much feeling, and that I was near crying at his pathos, and told him his 'verses were *terrible pretty*.' Nat said he would not have his uncle Richard see the poetry on any account, for he would be sure to laugh. I remember saying with much emphasis, that 'if his uncle said anything against the verses he was no judge.' We could not have been more than ten years old, and I suspect I was not an eminent critic; but it would be a satisfaction to hear those early productions of his read now, to know if they would touch the ear as they did then." [Symmes is mistaken as to the age of

Nat's po-etry.

the young poet ; he must have been fifteen years old, for the Tarbox tragedy
occurred March 17, 1819. The Knight
affair happened in 1807.]

"After the age of twenty I went to *Haw-*
sea, and have ever since been a wan- *thorne's*
derer, occasionally meeting Hawthorne *manner*
by chance. He never forgot me, and
once, after he graduated, came on board
a vessel in Salem harbor and stayed with
me two hours. I was then before the
mast. I . have heard people say Hawthorne was cold and distant ; if he was
so, there was one of his youthful associates who, as the world goes, was not
his equal socially, certainly not intel-
lectually, who was never forgotten. The
last time I saw him we were in Liverpool ; he recognized me across the street,
and 'hove me to.' We had a long talk,
and he conversed in that easy, bewitch-
ing style, of which he was perfect master when he pleased. I asked if he
had ever been to Raymond since his

mother moved back to Salem. He answered : —

" ' I have been there since, but have not a wish to go again, for soon after we left, uncle Richard rented the house to Colonel Eben Scribner, to keep a stage tavern ; everything I loved was neglected. Our fruit trees died, and the long row of butternuts that I watched with such solicitude are not inclosed, and now they have turned the old mansion into a meeting-house. Uncle Richard is dead, and little Betsey Tarbox is married and gone from there. No, my idols are destroyed, and I have no desire to revisit the places where the altars stood. But this I will tell you, that I have visited many places called beautiful in Europe and the United States, but have never seen the place that enchanted me like the flat rock at the outlet of Thomas Pond, from which we used to fish. In an October afternoon, just when the oak-trees put on their red coats, the view

FLAT ROCK, THOMAS POND

from that spot, looking to the slopes of Rattlesnake Mountain, through the haze of Indian summer, was to me more enchanting than anything I have since seen, and I have seriously thought of inducing some artist to go to Raymond in the pleasant autumn, to make for me a view from the rock where we used to play. I also wish that some curious person would open some of the Indian graves that I feel sure are there.'

"Hawthorne said much more that I cannot recall. I parted from him for the last time in Liverpool."

In further explanation of the misunderstanding in regard to the name, it *Change of name* should be said, that the family name was spelled *Hathorne* until 1825, when Nathaniel graduated. He had found that the proper spelling was *Hawthorne*, and himself made the change. In his diploma, giving the degree of Bachelor of Arts, the name was spelled without the "w," and on this parchment is still to be seen his partial erasure of the name as written by the college authorities, and his substitution of the new name he was to render famous.

Betsey Tarbox

All the names and incidents mentioned by Symmes have been verified, and a few years ago I found "little Betsey Tarbox," now a venerable matron. To her Hawthorne was only a family tradition, for she was only four or five years old when she last saw the lad who remembered her so fondly thirty years later. His aunt, who had been as a mother to her, often spoke of Nathaniel, and she had heard from her of the diary he left at Raymond. The letter from which the above extract is given was followed, at an interval of six months, by one in which the first intelligence of the diary was vouchsafed. I copy Symmes's account of the somewhat romantic way in which it came into his possession. He wrote, as before, from Alexandria, and signed only his initials : —

"Since the first year of the late war *First ac-*
I have been in this part of Virginia, and *count of*
in 1863 became acquainted with several *diary*
soldiers of the Twenty-fifth Maine Regiment, who were quartered in Fairfax
County. Among them was a private
named Small, to whom I rendered some
service during an illness, and was one
day inquiring what part of Cumberland
he came from, as I had been informed
that nearly all the regiment was raised
in that county. He said his home was
Raymond. I then asked him if he knew
that Hawthorne, the author, lived there
through his boyhood, but he seemed not
to understand my meaning. I then ex-
plained to him, but found he had never
heard of the man. After thinking a few
moments, he said, 'You remind me of
something; Frank Redo (the name as
well as I can spell and remember it)
moved a large lot of rich old furniture
from the old Manning house to the Captain Davis place several years ago. I

35

helped him to load and stow it away. There was a large mahogany bookcase and a lot of old books, and among them *The diary found* one entirely in writing, and I feel sure the name of Hawthorne was on the outside. I read portions, and it was a journal of some kind; it was filled with all sorts of *witch and ghost stories*, and a little of everything. Frank cared nothing for the book, and gave it to me. If no one has destroyed it, the thing is safe at home.'

" I said, if the book was what he described it would be a prize to me; and he promised if he got home alive he would certainly send it to me by express. Thinking that he would perhaps forget the matter, I forgot it myself, but in the latter part of 1864 it came to me at Camp Distribution, by the Sanitary Commission Express, neatly done up and directed. I have it now, and shall keep it while I keep anything. This book was originally a bound blank one, not ruled, and has been gnawed by mice or eaten by moths on the edges. On the first leaf, in a beautiful round hand, is written the following : —

" *'Presented by Richard Manning, to his* His un- *nephew Nathaniel Hathorne, with the advice* cle's gift *that he write out his thoughts, some every day, in as good words as he can, upon any and all subjects, as it is one of the best means of his securing for mature years, command of thought and language.*

" *'Raymond, June 1, 1816.'*

" The book has about two hundred and fifty pages, and was about six by eight inches before it was gnawed. It is writ- ten throughout, the first part in a boyish hand, though legibly, and showing in its progress a marked improvement in pen- manship.

" In his youth Hawthorne was much inclined to talk of the supernatural. I have heard him many times tell ghost Fond of and haunted house stories, though never ghost as though he believed what he was say- stories

37

ing. There always seemed to be an undercurrent of incredulity. One of your correspondents, who dates at Bolster's Mills [Robinson Cook], describes the mother of Nathaniel as being somewhat superstitious, and from what I recollect of her, he is correct. Not a gross and ignorant, but a polished and pious superstition. Perhaps this proclivity in the parent may account for his filling his journal with so many of the local stories of the supernatural.

"I am satisfied that the journal is a genuine one of Hawthorne's. Still it is possible that I have been imposed on, although I cannot conceive why or wherefore. As to selling the book, I should as soon think of making money on a favorite book bequeathed by my father. I think that there are entries in this manuscript book that will interest many readers, especially in the county of Cumberland. If it is spurious, there are many living who will detect it at once, for many things are noticed that must have at the time attained publicity. If you desire to publish some extracts from this journal, I will furnish them from time to time, my only object being to contribute a little in return for the pleasure I have enjoyed, through the kindness of a lady friend, in reading the 'Portland Transcript' for three years past."

Frank "Redo," to whom reference is *Francis* made in this letter, was either the *Radoux* Frenchman, Francis Radoux,[1] who married the widow of Richard Manning, or his son of the same name. The old gentleman was living in Portland when the above letter came to hand, and I called upon him, an officer of the Napoleonic wars, with whom I had long been ac-

[1] Francis Radoux came to this country soon after the downfall of Napoleon. At the battle of Waterloo he served as a lieutenant in the French army. He was a teacher of the polite accomplishment of dancing for many years in Portland and other New England cities. He died in Portland at a good old age, about twenty years ago. '

Had been told of diary quainted. He said that his wife had told him of this notebook, and wanted him to read it, but could not find it at the time, and believed it had been lost or loaned. He certainly had not given it to Small, and believed that Small had appropriated it at the time he assisted in removing his household goods from the Manning house, after the death of his wife. He admitted that it was possible his son had given it to Small. As for himself, he had never seen it.

It must be acknowledged that the mystery enveloping the whole affair up to this time made us suspicious that a literary hoax was being perpetrated. For not only had " W. S." failed to give any address by which he could be reached, but we could not find at Raymond or vicinity any one who could guess for whom the initials might stand. But when in a few weeks the first installment of the promised "extracts " came, with a letter signed "W. Sims," and still later other extracts followed; when we had learned the origin and history of our correspondent, and found his statements reliable in many instances, we could no longer doubt that the notes were really written by Hawthorne, and came to the conclusion that for some reason Symmes was afraid to trust the book out of his hands. Perhaps he feared that Small *Suspi-* did not come by it honestly, or that the *cions* Hawthorne family would claim it. The old Frenchman, Radoux, told me he should demand possession of it, if by any chance it came to light, as it had been left to him by his wife, Hawthorne's aunt. The Mannings in Salem were anxious to get it, in order to put at rest by the chirography the question of its genuineness. But all detective machin- *Detectives* ery set at work to find Symmes proved *employed* a failure, though I think we should have found him if we had known at the time that he was a colored man. When after his death this was made public, he was

41

remembered by many people in the home of his childhood. We found also a possible reason for the failure of the detectives who were employed at Washington in search of Symmes and the diary. Symmes *was himself a detective* in the very office to which application was made, and found some means to checkmate the searchers! He was a protégé and favorite of Colonel Baker.

The incidents and names recorded by Hawthorne in these notes have been verified by the memories of scores of our correspondents in Cumberland County. And even if it were not so, the internal evidence is convincing. The style is that of an immature Hawthorne, most clearly; and considering that he was only twelve years old when his uncle gave him the book, with the admirably expressed injunction to "write out his thoughts, some every day, in as good words as he could, upon any and all subjects," we think his first literary achievement remarkable. It

is a great pity that only a few of these *The book*
sibylline leaves have been rescued ; for *vanished*
Symmes died and the book vanished,
when he had copied only three install-
ments, comprising but comparatively few
of the two hundred and fifty pages of the
book. Symmes appears to have selected
for the most part the items that con-
tained names likely to be remembered in
the county. He gave us only one or
two of the creepy ghost stories of which
he speaks in his first account of the book.
As Symmes died in Pensacola, and probably had the book with him at the time,
a search in that region may yet reveal it.
It was a treasure this old playmate of
Hawthorne valued so highly that it is
most likely he would carry it with him in
his travels.

Julian Hawthorne, in his life of his
father, refers contemptuously to the
claims of this diary, and indeed affects
to consider it of little consequence even
if proved genuine. He says : —

Julian Haw- thorne's opinion

"With deference to the contrary opinion of those who are worth listening to on this subject, the present writer has been unable to find in this diary any trustworthy evidence, either external or internal, of its being anything else than a clumsy and leaky fabrication. Assuming it to be genuine, however, it seems singularly destitute of biographical value; and at all events it shall not be inflicted on the reader. . . . Babies are interesting and instructive in a high degree, because they are impersonal and unselfconscious; but a half-grown boy is a morally amphibious creature, who, so far as he has attained individuality, is disagreeable, and so far as he has not attained it, is superfluous."

I do not believe that this characterization of the extracts now to be given will be accepted as just criticism. These notes show the powers of close and minute observation which distinguished Hawthorne as a man and an author;

44

they were the work of a lad who had " attained individuality " without becoming " disagreeable." Mr. Lathrop, in his biographical sketch of his father-in-law, *Mr. Lathrop's belief* expresses belief in the genuineness of the diary, and copies a few of the items from it. But, as before remarked, no biographer of Hawthorne has taken sufficient account of his peculiar manner of life in the Maine wilderness, in its effect upon his susceptible nature. None of them seems to understand how much of his boyhood and young manhood was spent there. It may be that his mother did not occupy the house her brother built for her later than the year 1822, but Nathaniel made his home with his uncle during his visits in other years. His college and his Raymond home were only a few miles apart. No biography mentions the fact that for at least one term Hawthorne's studies in preparation for college were prosecuted at Stroudwater, Westbrook, which is also in Cumberland County. He went from Raymond with Jacob Dingley, a relative of Mrs. Manning's, whom Hawthorne mentions in his diary, and they lived in *Rev. Caleb* the family of their teacher, Rev. Caleb *Bradley* Bradley, who was a graduate of Harvard, somewhat. eccentric, and a man of such pronounced individuality that it would be strange if even the few weeks Hawthorne spent with him did not leave lasting impressions upon his mind. And yet I fail to find any reference to this teacher in any work of Hawthorne's, unless it be in The Vision of the Fountain in " Twice - Told Tales." In this sketch he locates himself in a village more than a hundred miles from home, at the age of fifteen, and living in the family of an old clergyman, who economizes fuel by using, as the foundation of his parlor fire, a heap of tan, or ground bark. All these circumstances seem a reminiscence of his brief residence at Stroudwater, while a pupil of Bradley's.

The first installment of extracts sent by Symmes was accompanied by a note dated at Alexandria, Virginia, January 21, 1871, and signed " W. Sims," this being the first hint of the name of our correspondent. In this note he said : —

" I have copied exactly some of the *Symmes's* entries in Hawthorne's journal, and send *third* them to you herewith. They are no *letter* doubt genuine, or if they are not, your readers in that region will detect the fraud. I know not whether the names are real or fictitious ; only two of them were known to me thirty-six years ago. Almost all the dates in the journal are gone. They were close to the margin, and mice and moths have eaten the outer edges. The book has at some time been in the water so as to destroy the binding and obliterate every date on the inner right hand margin. If what I send are not worth publishing, burn them ; if they are, and you hereafter signify in ' notices to correspondents ' that you would like more extracts, when I have time I will send some additional. What I here send were copied whenever I could get a few spare moments. As I shall always remember Cumberland County with pleasure, if the extracts shall amuse any of your readers there I shall be well paid."

Having now given a history of the diary, some romantic features of which at first excited suspicion, we will set forth the "extracts" sent by Symmes, confident that unprejudiced readers will agree with us that whatever may be said of the external evidence, the internal is satisfactory proof that they came from the hand of Hawthorne. Within a few weeks after the publication of the notes, we received scores of letters confirmatory of the names and incidents mentioned, some of the most striking of these verifications coming after we had learned of the death of Symmes. The notes are here given exactly as received, with the addition of some explanations and corroboratory circumstances.

CHAPTER III

EXTRACTS FROM DIARY

WENT yesterday in a sailboat on *A sail* the Great Pond with Mr. Peter *on Lake* White,[1] of Windham. He sailed up here *Sebago* from White's Bridge to see Captain Dingley, and invited Joseph Dingley and Mr. Ring to take a boat-ride out to the Dingley Islands and to the Images. He was also kind enough to say that I might go, with my mother's consent, which she gave after much coaxing. Since the loss of my father, she dreads to have any one belonging to her go upon the water. It is strange that this beautiful body of water is called a "Pond." The geo-

[1] [Peter White was long considered the best pilot of Sebago Lake, and of Songo and Crooked rivers, in which region he spent much of his life fishing and fowling. The common name of the lake at that time was "Great Pond."]

graphy tells of many in Scotland and Ireland, not near so large, that are called "Lakes." It is not respectful to speak of so noble, deep, and broad a collection of clear water as a "Pond." It makes a stranger think of geese, and then of goosepond. Mr. White, who knows all this region, told us that the streams from thirty-five ponds, large and small, flow into this, as he calls it, Great Basin. We landed on one of the small islands that Captain Dingley cleared for a sheep pasture when he first came to Raymond. Mr. Ring said he had to do it to keep his sheep from the bears and wolves. A growth of trees has started on the island, and makes a grove so fine and pleasant, that I wish almost that our house was there. On the way from the island to the Images, Mr. Ring caught a black spotted trout that was almost a whale, and weighed, before it was cut open, after we got back to uncle Richard's store, eighteen and a half pounds.

The men said that if it had been weighed
as soon as it came out of the water it
would have been nineteen pounds. This
trout had a droll-looking hooked nose,
and they tried to make me believe that
if the line had been in my hands I should
have been obliged to let go, or have been
pulled out of the boat. They were men,
and had a right to say so. I am a boy,
and have a right to think differently.
We landed at the Images, when I crept *In cave*
into the cave and got a drink of cool *at " The*
water. In coming home we sailed over *Images "*
a place, not far from the Images, where
Mr. White has at some time let down a
line four hundred feet without finding .
bottom. This seems strange, for he told
us, too, that his boat, as it floated, was
only two hundred and fifty feet higher
than the boats in Portland Harbor, and
that if the Great Pond was pumped dry,
a man standing on its bottom, just under
where we then were, would be more than
one hundred and fifty feet lower than

the surface of the water at the Portland wharves. Coming up the Dingley Bay,

Rattle-snake Moun-tain

had a good view of Rattlesnake Mountain, and it seemed to me wonderfully beautiful as the almost setting sun threw over its western crags streams of fiery light. If the Indians were very fond of this part of the country, it is easy to see why. Beavers, otters, and the finest fish were abundant, and the hills and streams furnished constant variety. I should have made a good Indian if I had been born in a wigwam. To talk like sailors, we "made" the old hemlock stub, at the mouth of the Dingley Brook, just before sunset, and sent a *boy* ashore with a hawser, and were soon safely moored to a bunch of alders. After we got ashore,

Firing long gun

Mr. White allowed me to fire his long gun at a mark. I did not hit the mark, and am not sure that I saw it at the time the gun went off, but believe rather that I was watching for the noise that I was about to make. Mr. Ring said that

52

with practice I could be a gunner, and that now, with a very heavy charge, he thought I could kill a horse at eight paces! Mr. White went to uncle Richard's for the night, and I went home, and amused my mother with telling how pleasantly the day had passed. When I told her what Mr. Ring said about my killing a horse, she said he was making fun of me. I had found that out before.

SWAPPED pocket-knives with Robinson Cook yesterday. Jacob Dingley says that he cheated me; but I think not, for I cut a fishing-pole this morning, and did it well. Besides, he is a Quaker, and they never cheat. *Swapping knives*

[Robinson Cook and Jacob Dingley were both living when this item was printed. Mr. Cook wrote: "There can be no doubt of the truth of Nat's records, nor has he used any fictitious names.

I did not at first distinctly recollect of swapping knives with him, but, after considering, the whole affair is fresh in my mind. I do not recollect how we traded; but as he and Jacob Dingley were great cronies, and were ever trying in a jocose manner to 'trig each other's wheels,' it seems that Jacob tried to irritate Nat on this occasion by telling him that he had got cheated."]

King-birds

TWO kingbirds have built their nest between our house and the mill-pond. The male is more courageous than any creature that I know about. He seems to have taken possession of the territory from the great pond to the small one, and goes out to war with every fish-hawk that flies from one to the other over his dominion. The fish-hawks must be miserable cowards to be driven by such a speck of a bird. I have not yet seen one turn to defend himself.

CAPTAIN BRITTON, from Otis- *Britton's* field, was at uncle Richard's to- *joke* day. Not long ago uncle brought here from Salem a new kind of potatoes, called "Long Reds." Captain Britton had some for seed, and uncle asked how he liked them. He answered, " They yield well, grow very long; one end is very poor, and the other good for nothing." I laughed about it after he was gone; but uncle looked sour, and said there was no wit in his answer, and that the saying was stale. It was new to me, and his way of saying it very funny. Perhaps uncle did not like to hear his favorite potato spoken of in that way, and that if the captain had praised it he would have been called witty. Captain Britton promised to bring "Gulliver's Travels " for me to read, the next time he goes to Portland. Uncle Richard has not the book in his library.

Mother's fears

THIS morning the bucket got off the chain and dropped back into the well. I wanted to go down on the stones and get it. Mother would not consent, for fear the wall might cave in, but hired Samuel Shane to go down. In the goodness of her heart, she thought the son of old Mrs. Shane not quite so valuable as the son of the widow Hathorne. God bless her for all her love for me, though it may be some selfish. We are to have a pump in the well after this mishap.

An expert drummer

WASHINGTON LONGLEY has been taking lessons of a drumming master. He was in the grist-mill to-day, and practiced with two sticks on the half bushel. I was astonished at the great number of strokes in a second; and if I had not seen that he had but two sticks, should have supposed he was drumming with twenty.

MAJOR BERRY went past our *Buying a* house with a large drove of sheep *lamb* yesterday. One, a last spring's lamb, gave out, — could go no further. I saw him down near the bridge. The poor dumb creature looked into my eyes, and I thought I knew what he would say if he could speak, and so asked Mr. Berry what he would sell him for. "Just the price of his pelt, and that will bring sixty-five cents," was the answer. I ran and petitioned mother for the money, which she soon gave me, saying, with a smile, that she tried to make severe, but could not, that I was "a great spend-thrift." The lamb is in our orchard now, and he made a bow (without taking off his hat), and thanked me this morning for saving him from the butcher.

[The late Hon. William Goold, of Windham, the historian, wrote to me this comment upon the above item: "Major Berry, the drover, passed my home on his way to market with his droves of tired lambs, in the heat of July and August, regularly for several years. I have often felt as Hawthorne did when they gave out on the road, and would have gladly purchased one if I had had the money. Mr. Berry was a short, fleshy man, and always rode horseback, apparently suffering as much in the sun as the lambs."]

Rattle-snakes

MR. MARCH GAY killed a rattlesnake yesterday, not far from his house, that was more than six feet long, and had twelve rattles. This morning, Mr. Jacob Mitchell killed another near the same place, almost as long. It is supposed they were a pair, and that the second one was on the track of its mate. If every rattle counts a year, the first one was twelve years old. Eliakim Maxfield came down to mill to-day, and told me about the snakes.

58

MR. HENRY TURNER, of Otis-   *Bear*
field, took his axe and went out   *story*
between Saturday and Moose ponds, to
look at some pine-trees. A rain had just
taken off enough of the snow to lay bare
the roots of a part of the trees. Under
a large root there seemed to be a cavity,
and on examining closely, something was
exposed very much like long black hair.
He cut off the root, saw the nose of a
bear, and killed him, pulled out the body,
saw another, killed that, and dragged out
its carcass, when he found that there was
a third one in the den, and that he was
thoroughly awake, too ; but as soon as
the head came in sight, it was split open
with the axe, so that Mr. Turner alone,
with only an axe, killed three bears in
less than half an hour, the youngest being
a good-sized one, and what the hunters
call a yearling. This is a pretty great
bear story, but probably true, and happened only a few weeks ago ; for John
Patch, who was here with his father, Cap-

tain Levi Patch, who lives within two miles of the Saturday Pond, told me so yesterday.

[Robinson Cook informed me that the bear story here related was true, in the main. Turner went to the woods with his oxen to get birch bark to make sap buckets. His dog discovered the den of bears, and two were killed with the axe. The third was wounded with the same weapon, and retreated to the farthest side of the den, where he could not be reached. Turner finally dispatched him with a long, sharpened stake. His oxen were so badly frightened, that he was obliged to fasten them to a tree with chains until he had loaded the dead bears upon his sled. Then he let the oxen loose, jumped upon the sled, and was carried home at a furious pace by the maddened animals.]

A YOUNG man named Henry Jackson, Jr., was drowned two days ago, up in Crooked River. He and one of his friends were trying which could swim the faster. Jackson was behind but gaining; his friend kicked at him in fun, thinking to hit his shoulder and push him back, but missed, and hit his chin, which caused him to take in water and strangle, and before his friend could help or get help, poor Jackson was (Elder Leach says) "beyond the reach of mercy." I read one of the Psalms to my mother this morning, and it plainly declares *Elder* twenty-six times, that "God's mercy endureth forever." I never saw Henry *Leach criticised* Jackson, — he was a young man just married. Mother is sad; says she shall not consent to my swimming any more in the mill-pond, with the boys, fearing that in sport my mouth might get kicked open, and then sorrow for a dead son be added to that for my dead father, which she says would break her heart. I love

61

to swim, but shall not disobey my mother.

Kind heart but hard creed

[Robinson Cook, upon the publication of the above item, wrote to me as follows : " I remember well almost every circumstance related by Nat, and especially the death and funeral of Henry Jackson, Jr. ; I was at the funeral. Elder Leach preached the sermon, and such were the circumstances of his death, that he could not, according to his creed, find a happy resting-place for poor Henry in that country from which no traveler returns. I helped carry the remains to the silent grave, and very many hearts were sad on considering, as Elder Leach said, that he was ' out of the reach of mercy ; ' hence the sadness of Mrs. Hawthorne, when she called upon her son to read the psalm he mentions. Elder Leach was a Freewill Baptist minister, with a kind, sympathizing heart, and ready on all occasions to visit the sick, attend all funerals in his precinct, and do this without pay; but a hard creed lay in the way of his tender and Christian emotions."]

I CAN from my chamber window look *Betty* across into aunt Manning's garden, *Tarbox* this morning, and see little Betty Tar-box, flitting among the rosebushes, and in and out of the arbor, like a tiny witch. She will never realize the calamity that came upon her brothers and sisters, that terrible night when her father and mother lay within a few rods of each other, in the snow, freezing to death. I love the elf, because of her loss; and still my aunt is much more to her than her own mother, in her poverty, could have been.

[This item, if accepted as genuine, con-clusively proves that the Hawthornes were living in their house across the creek from the Mannings in the summer of 1819. Nathaniel's chamber window did not look *down* into, but *across* into, his aunt's garden. The residences were separated by a narrow stream. I have heard, but cannot now verify the statement, that the ledger kept in a store in that vicinity shows an account with the Hawthornes, who must have been keeping house by themselves in Raymond, in the summer of 1822, the year after Hawthorne entered college. At all events, he spent his vacations here, either with his mother or his uncle. There were five children orphaned by the death of Mr. and Mrs. Tarbox. The story of the great storm, in which they lost their lives, has in it such elements of pathos that it is here given, to account for young Hawthorne's deep interest, as shown in this note and in the narrative by Symmes:

Story of Tarbox tragedy In the second week of March, 1819, a severe snowstorm began, which lasted nine days, and the cold was intense. There being no food in the house, Mr.

64

Tarbox went five miles for a supply, and upon his return found the drifts so deep that he had not the strength to get through them with his load. When not far from his home he left the bag of provisions upon a tree, and tried to reach his door, but soon sank down exhausted. His calls for help were heard by his wife, who went to his assistance. She covered him with her shawl, and realizing the necessities of her starving family, attempted to get the food he had left behind. But the drifts were too deep, and the cold too intense. She sank down and perished near the tree, while her husband was dying close to their home. Their bodies were found two days afterward. Mrs. Manning adopted Betsey, the youngest of the orphaned children, aged four.]

FISHING from the bridge to-day, I *Big eel* caught an eel two thirds as long as myself. Mr. Watkins tried to make me believe that he thought it a water-moccasin snake. Old Mr. Shane said that it was a "young sea sarpint, sure." Mr. Fickett, the blacksmith, begged it to take home for its skin, as he said for buskin strings and flail strings. So ends my day's fishing.

Bricks without straw

WENT over to-day to see Watkins make bricks. I have always thought there was some mystery about it, but I can make them myself. Why did the Israelites complain so much at having to make bricks without straw? I should not use straw if I was a brick-maker; besides, when they are burned in the kiln, the straw will burn out, and leave the bricks full of holes.

Polly Maxfield

POLLY MAXFIELD came riding to mill to-day on horseback. She rode gracefully as a trooper. I wish with

66

all my heart that I was as daring a rider, or half so graceful.

[Robinson Cook says of the mill, so *The* often referred to in these notes, that it *Dingley* was known as the old Dingley mill, and *mill* was built in 1772. A grant of one hundred acres of land was made to Joseph Dingley, its builder. His son, Samuel Dingley, was the miller of Hawthorne's time, and he was then old and crippled. "This mill," says Cook, "was situated near the home of Mrs. Hawthorne. To this mill came all sorts of customers, from a five franc piece to a fourpence ha'penny, — men, women, and children, some on foot, who would bring their grist to mill ten miles. Nearly all came on horseback. Polly Maxfield was the eldest daughter of her father's family, and a sister of Eliakim, the well-known stage driver from Waterford to Portland for about thirty years."]

An ill-used horse

THIS morning I saw at the grist-mill a solemn-faced old horse, hitched to the trough. He had brought for his owner some bags of corn to be ground, who, after carrying them into the mill, walked up to uncle Richard's store, leaving his half-starved animal in the cold wind, with nothing to eat, while the corn was being turned to meal. I felt sorry, and nobody being near, thought it best to have a talk with the old nag, and said, "Good-morning, Mr. Horse, how are you to-day?" "Good-morning, youngster," said he, just as plain as a horse can speak, and then said, "I am almost dead, and I wish I was quite. I am hungry, have had no breakfast, and must stand here tied by the head while they are grinding the corn, and until master drinks two or three glasses of rum at the store, and then drag him and the meal up the Ben Ham hill, and home, and am now so weak that I can hardly stand. Oh, dear, I am in a bad way," and the old creature cried — I almost cried myself.

Just then the miller went downstairs to the meal trough. I heard his feet on the steps, and, not thinking much what I was doing, ran into the mill, and taking the four quart toll-dish nearly full of corn out of the hopper, carried it out and poured it into the trough before the horse, and placed the dish back before the miller came up from below. When I got out, the horse was laughing, but he had to eat slowly, because the bits were *Relief* in his mouth. I told him that I was *offered* sorry, but did not know how to take them out, and should not dare to, if I did, for his master might come out of the store suddenly and see what I was about. "Thank you," said he, "a luncheon of corn with the bits in is much better than none. The worst of it is, I have to munch so slowly, that my master may come before I finish it, and thrash me for eating his corn, and you for your kindness." I sat down on a stone out of the wind, and waited in trouble, for fear that the miller or the owner of the corn would come and find out what I had done. At last the horse winked and stuck out his upper lip ever so far, and then said, "The last kernel is gone;" then he laughed a little, then shook one ear, then the other, then shut his eyes as if to take a nap. I jumped up and said, "How do you feel, old fellow; any better?" He opened his eyes, and, looking at me kindly, answered, "Very much," and then blew his nose exceedingly loud, but he did not wipe it; perhaps he had no wiper. I then asked if *The iron* his master whipped him. "Not much *brad* lately; he used to, till my hide got hardened, but now he has a white oak goad stick with an iron brad in its end, with which he jabs my hind quarters, and hurts me awfully." I asked why he did not kick up, and knock his tormentor out of the wagon. "I did try to once," said

70

he, "but am old and was weak, and could only get my heels high enough to break the whiffletree, and besides lost my balance and fell down flat. Master then jumped down, and, getting a cudgel, struck me over the head, and I thought my troubles were over. This happened just before Mr. Ben Ham's house, and I should have been finished, and ready for the crows, if he had not stepped out and told master not to strike again, if he did· he would shake his liver out. That saved my life; but I was sorry, though Mr. Ham meant good."

The goad with the iron brad was in *"Old* the wagon, and, snatching it out, I struck *colt"* the end against a stone, and the stabber *grateful* flew into the mill-pond. "There," says I, "old colt," as I threw the goad back into the wagon, "he won't harpoon you again with *that* iron." The poor old brute knew what I said well enough, for I looked him in the eye and spoke horse language. So he turned his long upper lip away back and laughed again, I thought a *little* exultingly. Very soon, however, a tear came into his eye, and he said, "My young friend, do you know how long horses live?" I answered that I had heard that some lived thirty years. "Oh, dear!" said he, "I am sorry. I am twenty-four, and have been hoping that I should die before snow fell; it does not seem that I can possibly go through another winter," and the tears began to run again.

At that moment the brute that owned the horse came out of the store and down the hill towards us. I slipped behind a pile of slabs. The meal was put in the wagon, the horse unhitched, the wagon mounted, the goad picked up, and a thrust made; but Dobbin was in no hurry. Looking at the end of his stick, the man bawled, "What little devil has had my gourd?" and then began striking with all his strength; but his steed only walked, shaking his head as he went across the bridge, and I thought I heard the ancient Equus say as he went, "Thrash as much as you please; for once you cannot stab." I went home *Case of* a little uneasy, not feeling sure that the *conscience* feeding the man's corn to his own horse was not stealing, and thinking that if the miller found it out he would have me taken down before Squire Longley.

[Mr. Lathrop copies part of the above extract in a sketch of his father-in-law, and says of it that "it is the first instance on record of a mild approach of Hawthorne to writing fiction." Robinson Cook informs me that he recognizes the portraits of the hard master and the ill-used horse. Of the master, he says: "He was a worthless, tyrannical, cruel man, past middle age, with a large family of boys and girls, who had to look out for themselves when of age sufficient. He and his son would come together to mill. I have seen them occasionally at

73

the store. In bitter cold days the horse would have to stand without covering, while the northern blast was whistling through his hair and over the chafed places worn tender by the old harness. Without food or shelter he would have to remain, while father and son played cards in the store to decide which should pay for the drinks."]

At Pulpit Rock THIS morning walked down to the Pulpit Rock hill, and climbed up into the pulpit. It looks like a rough place to preach from, and does not seem so much like a pulpit when one is in it as when viewing it from the road below. It is a wild place, and really a curiosity. I brought a book, and sat in the rocky recess and read nearly an hour. This is a point on the road known to all teamsters. They have a string of names for reference, by which they tell each other where they met fellow-teamsters, or where their loads got stuck, and I have learned them from those who stop for drinks at the store. One meets another near our house and says, "Where did you meet Bill —— ?" "Just this side of Small's Brook," or "At the top of Gay's Pinch," "At the Dry Millpond," "Just the other side of Lemmy Jones's," "On the Long Causeway," "At Jeems Gowen's," "Coming down the Pulpit Rock hill," "Coming down Tarkill hill." I have heard these answers till I have them by heart, without having any idea where any of the places are, excepting the one I have seen to-day. While on the bridge, near the pulpit, Mr. West, who lives not far away, came along and asked where I had been. On my telling him, he said no money would hire him to go up to that pulpit; that the devil used *Devil* to preach from it to the Indians long, *preaches* long ago; that on a time when hundreds *to In-* of them were listening to one of his ser- *dians* mons, a great chief laughed in the devil's

75

face, upon which he stamped his foot, and the ground to the southwest, where they were standing, sank fifty feet, and every Indian went down out of sight, leaving a swamp to this day. He declared that he once stuck a pole in there, which went down easily several feet, but then struck the skull bone of an Indian, when instantly all the hassocks and flags began to shake, and he heard a yell as from fifty overgrown Pequots; that he left the hole and ran for life, and would not go to the bog again for the best farm in Raymond. Mr. West also said that no Indian had ever been known to go near that swamp since, but that whenever one came that way, he turned out of the road near the house of Mr. West, and went straight to Thomas Pond, keeping to the eastward of the Pulpit Rock, giving it a "wide berth." Mr. West talked as though he believed what he said.

Mr. West's legend

A PEDDLER, named Dominicus Jor- *A ghost* dan, was to-day in uncle Rich- *story* ard's store, telling a ghost story. I listened intently, but tried not to seem interested. The story was of a house, the owner of which was suddenly killed. Since his death, the west garret window cannot be kept closed, though the shutters be hasped and nailed at night; they are invariably found open the next morning, and no one can tell when or how the nails are drawn. There is also on the farm an apple-tree, of the fruit of which the owner was particularly fond, but since his death no person has been able to get one of the apples. The tree hangs full nearly every year; but whenever any individual tries to get one, stones come in all directions, as if thrown from some secret, infernal battery, or hidden catapult, and more than once have those making the attempt been struck. What is more strange, the tree stands in an open field, there being no shelter near from which tricks can be played without exposure. Jordan says that it seems odd to strangers to see that tree loaded with apples when the snow is four feet deep; and, what is a mystery, there are no apples in the spring; no one ever sees the wind blow one off, none are ever seen on the snow, nor even the vestige of one on the grass under the tree; and that children may play under and around it while it is in blossom, and until the fruit is large enough to tempt them, with perfect safety. *Bewitched* But the moment one of the apples is *apple-tree* sought for, the air is full of flying stones. He further says that late one starlight night, he was passing the house, and, looking up, saw the phantom walk out of the garret window, with cane in hand, making all the motions, as if walking on *terra firma*, although what appeared to be his feet were at least six yards from the ground, and so he went walking away on nothing; and, when nearly out of sight, there was a great flash and an explosion as of twenty fieldpieces—then —nothing! This story was told with seeming earnestness, and listened to as though it was believed. How strange it is that almost all persons, old or young, are fond of hearing about the supernatural, though it produces nervousness, and often fear. I should not be willing to sleep in that garret, though I do not believe a word of the story.

[Dominicus Jordan was a peddler who made his circuit in Cumberland County. After acquiring a small fortune at this business, he went west, became wealthy, and died in Wisconsin in 1869. In his story of "Mr. Higginbotham's Catastrophe," Hawthorne introduces the character of *Dominicus* Pike, the Yankee tobacco peddler, whose name, unusual in New England, was evidently suggested by that of the Raymond peddler whose story of the bewitched apple-tree is here recorded.]

THE lumbermen from Saccarappa are getting their logs across the Great Pond. Yesterday a strong northwest wind blew a great raft of many thousands over almost to the mouth of the Dingley Brook. Their anchor dragged for more than a mile, but when the boom was within twenty or thirty rods of the shore, it brought up and held, as I heard some men say who are familiar with such business. All the men and boys went from the mill down to the pond to see the great raft, and I among them. They have a string of logs fastened end to end and surrounding the great body, which keeps them from scattering; and the string is called a boom. A small strong raft, it may be forty feet square, with an upright windlass in its centre, called a capstan, is fastened to some part of the boom. The small raft is called "head works," and from it, in a yawl boat, is carried the anchor, to which is attached a strong rope half a mile long. The boat is rowed out the whole length of the rope, the anchor thrown over, and the men on the "head works" wind up the capstan, and so draw along the acres of logs. After we got down to the shore, several of the men came out on the boom nearest to us, and striking a single log, pushed it under and outside. Then one man, with a gallon jug slung to his back, taking a pickpole, pushed himself ashore on the small single *Riding a* log, — a feat that seemed almost miracu- *single* lous to me. This man's name was Reu- *log* ben March, and he seemed to be in no fear of getting soused, though the top of the log was but just out of water. This masterly kind of navigation he calls " cuffing the rigging." Nobody could tell me why he gave it that name. March went up to the store, and had the jug filled with rum (the supply having run out on the head works), and made the voyage back in the way he came. His comrades received him with cheers,

and after sinking the log and drawing it
back under the boom, proceeded to try
the contents of the jug, seeming to be
well satisfied with the result of his expedition. It turned out that March only
rode the single log ashore to show his
adroitness, for the yawl boat soon came
round from the head works, and brought
near a dozen men, in red shirts, to where
we were. I was interested listening to
their conversation, mixed with sharp
jokes. Nearly every one had a nick-
name. March, who came after the rum,
was " Captain Snarl ; " a tall, fierce looking man, who had just filled my idea of a
Spanish freebooter, was " Doctor Coodle." I think his real name was Wood.
The rum seemed to make them crazy,
for one who was called " Rub-a-Dub "
pitched Doctor Coodle, head and heels,
into the water. A gentlemanly man
named Thompson, who acted as master
of ceremonies, or Grand Turk, interfered
and put a stop to what was becoming

*Nick-
names*

82

something like a fight. Mr. Thompson said that the wind would go down with the sun, and that they must get ready to start. This morning I went down to look for them, and the raft was almost to Frye's Island.

I HAVE read "Gulliver's Travels," *Lies too* and do not agree with Captain Brit- *false* ton that it is a witty and uncommonly interesting book. The wit is obscene, and the *lies too false*.

[The extracts given above were all that were ever received directly from Symmes. But nearly two years after his death we received from one Dickinson, of Alexandria, a package which he informed us was found among the papers of Symmes, left behind when he went to Pensacola, where he died. He had copied out a longer sketch than any previously furnished, which is given below, and it is the only one of the whole series which is dated. Dickinson was as provokingly careful as had been Symmes to give no address by *Another* which we could reach him. His note *Virginia* indicated that he was a friend of Symmes, *corre-* but whether or not he was of the same *spondent* race could not be ascertained. Hoping that we might learn from him still more about the journal, no effort was spared to find him; but Dickinson proved as elusive as his friend, and we never again heard from him. If Hawthorne's style had not been so evident in every one of these notes, if other internal and external evidence had not been so strong, the mysterious avoidance of our two Virginia correspondents of everything that might have given a clue to their personality would have been regarded as fatally suspicious. But the hand of the young master, as revealed in these lines, was one that could not be counterfeited by comparatively illiterate men. Some one wrote these notes who was not only thoroughly familiar with Raymond and its people, but who was already in command of a literary style decidedly Hawthornesque. The entry in the journal now to be given is full of allusions to people well known in Cumberland County. Several of them were personally known to the present writer, and the characteristics recorded fit them remarkably well. It is not an unnatural suggestion, considering the elements of mystery surrounding the matter, that some one was for two years engaged in working up a literary hoax. But if that were the case, it is evident that a person capable of writing these notes, expecting to get any sport or reputation out of his work, could have attained his object only by eventually showing his hand. No money *No money* was ever called for, though offered in *asked for* many ways and at many times. More than a quarter of a century of silence and corroboratory circumstances without number force the conclusion that we have before us a genuine work of one of the greatest artists in words of his time. The letter from Dickinson, mentioned above, I have mislaid, and his Christian name I have forgotten, but have the impression it was Charles. I remember that it claimed to be from a friend of Symmes, and it mentioned the fact that Symmes died in Florida, probably having the notebook with him. *Who was* Dickinson also said that when Symmes *Dickin-* was copying the extracts from the note-*son ?* book, his right arm was disabled, and that he (Dickinson) had acted as his amanuensis. This accounted for the fact, which otherwise would have puzzled us, that the handwritings of Symmes and Dickinson were so much alike as they certainly were. They both wrote with pencil and not with ink, and the chirography was remarkably good. I mention this singular circumstance in order to include every element of suspicion. My present belief is that Dickinson was associated with Symmes as a member of Baker's detectives, not in the regular force, but employed to spy upon the regulars. In this occupation they made enemies, and felt obliged to keep in hiding, even after the war was over. This is hinted at in the obituary notice of Symmes given in the Postscript. This notice was probably written by Dickinson, whoever Dickinson might be.]

DAY before yesterday, Mr. Thomas *Invited* Little, from Windham Hill, Mr. *to sail on* M. P. Sawyer, of Portland, Mr. Thomas *Sebago* A. Deblois, a lawyer, Mr. Hanson, of Windham, and Enoch White, a boy of my own age, from White's Bridge, came up to the Dingley Brook in a sailboat. They were on the way to Muddy River bog, for a day's sport, fishing and shooting ducks. Enoch proposed that I should go with them. I needed no urging, but knew how unwillingly my mother would consent. They could wait but a few minutes, and uncle Richard kindly wrote a note, asking her to be willing to gratify me *this time*.

She said, "Yes," but I was almost sorry, knowing that my day's pleasure would cost *her* one of anxiety. However, I gathered up hooks and lines, with some white salted pork for bait, and with a fabulous number of biscuit, split in the middle, the insides well buttered, then skillfully put together again, and all stowed in sister's large work-bag, and *Bet with* slung over my shoulder, I started, mak-*Enoch* ing a wager with Enoch White, as we *White* walked down to the boat, as to which would catch the largest number of fish.

The air was clear, with just breeze enough to shoot us along pleasantly, without making rough waves. The wind was not exactly after us, though we made but two tacks to reach the mouth of *The* Muddy River. The men praised the *scenery* grand view, after we got into the Great

THOMAS POND, RATTLESNAKE MOUNTAIN IN THE DISTANCE.

Bay. We could see the White Hills to the northwest, though Mr. Little said they were eighty miles from us, and grand old Rattlesnake to the northeast, in its immense jacket of green oak, looked more inviting than I had ever seen it, while Frye's Island, with its close growth of great trees, growing to the very edge of the water, looked like a monstrous green raft, floating to the southeastward. Whichever way the eye turned, something charming appeared.

Mr. Little seems to be familiar with every book that has ever been written, and must have a great memory. Among other things, he said : —

" Gentlemen, do you know that this *Mr. Lit-* should be called the sea instead of the *tle's talk* Great Pond; that ships should be built here, and navigate this water ? The surface of the Sea of Galilee, of which we read so much in the New Testament, was just about equal to the surface of our sea to-day."

And then he went on to give a geographical description of the country about the Sea of Galilee, and draw parallels between places named in the Testament and points in sight. His talk stole my attention until we were fairly at Muddy River mouth.

Muddy River bog Muddy River bog is quite a curiosity. The river empties into the pond between two small, sandy capes or points, only a short distance apart; but after running up a little between them, we found the bog to widen to fifty or sixty rods in some places, and to be between two and three miles long. People say that it has no bottom, and that the longest pole that ever grew may be run down into the mud, and then pushed down with another, a little longer, and this may be repeated till the long poles are all gone.

Coarse, tall water-grass grows up from the mud, over every part, with the exception of a space five or six rods wide, running its whole length, and nearly in the middle, which is called the channel. One can tell at first sight that it is the place for pickerel and water-snakes.

Mr. Deblois stated something that I never heard before as a fact in natural history : that the pickerel wages war on all fishes except the trout, who is too active for him ; that he is a piscatorial cannibal ; but that under all circumstances, and in all places, he lives on good terms with the water-snakes.

We saw a great many ducks, but they seemed to know that Mr. Sawyer had a gun, and flew on slight notice. At last, as four were flying, and seemed to be entirely out of gunshot, he fired, saying he would frighten them, if no more, when, to our surprise, he brought one down. The gun was loaded with ball, and Mr. Deblois told him that he could not do it again in a million times. Mr. Sawyer laughed, saying that he had always been a votary of chance, and that, as a general thing, she had treated him handsomely. *A votary of chance*

We sailed more than a mile up the bog, fishing and trolling for pickerel, and though we saw a great many, not one offered to be caught; but hornpouts were willing, and we caught them till it *The jews'-* was no sport. We found a man there *harp man* who had taken nearly two bushels of pouts. He was on a raft, and had walked from near the foot of Long Pond, in Otisfield. Mr. Little knew him, and intending to have some fun, said: —

"The next time you come to Portland I want half a dozen of your best jews'-harps; leave them at my store at Windham hill; I need them very badly."

The man deliberately took from the hook a large pout that he had just pulled up, and, laying his fishing-pole down, began to explore solemnly in his pockets, and brought out six giant jews'-harps carefully tied to pieces of corncob. Then he tossed them into our boat to Mr. Little, saying, "There they are, Tom, and they are as good ones as I ever made; I shall charge you fifty cents for them."

Mr. Little had the worst of the joke, but as the other men began to rally him, he took out the silver and paid the half-dollar; but they laughed at him till he told them if they would say no more about it, he would give them all the brandy they could drink when they got home.

Mr. Deblois said he would not be *Too good* bribed, and that he must tell Peter *to keep* White, when he got to Windham hill.

Mr. Little said he would not have Peter White know it for a yoke of steers.

After fishing till all were tired, we landed on a small dry knoll, that made out into the bog, to take our luncheon. The men had a variety of eatables, and *The* several bottles that held no eatables. *luncheon* The question was started whether Enoch and I should be invited to drink, and they concluded not to urge us as we were boys, and under their care; so Mr.

Deblois said, "Boys, anything to eat that is in our baskets is as much yours as ours,—help yourselves; but we shall not invite you to drink spirits."

We thanked them and said we had plenty of our own to eat, and had no relish for spirits, but were very thirsty for water. Mr. Little had been there before, and directed us to a spring of the best of water, that boiled up like a pot from the ground just at the margin of the bog.

Settling the bet

Before starting to return, the bet between Enoch and myself had to be settled. By the conditions, the one who caught the largest number of fish was to have all the hooks and lines of the other. I counted my string, and found twenty-five; Enoch made twenty-six on his. So I was about turning over the spoils when Mr. Sawyer said my string was the largest — that there was a mistake. So he counted and made twenty-six on mine, and twenty-five on Enoch's. We

94

counted again, and found it was as he said; and Enoch prepared to pay the bet, when Mr. Sawyer again interfered, saying that Enoch's string was certainly larger than mine, and proposed to count again. This time I had twenty-four, and Enoch twenty-seven. All the men counted them several times over, and until we could not tell which was which, and they never came out twice alike.

At length Mr. Deblois said with so- *Sawyer's* lemnity, "Stop this, Sawyer; you have *sleight of* turned these fish into a pack of cards, *hand* and are fooling us all." The men laughed heartily, and so should I if I had known what the point of the joke was. Mr. Deblois said that the decision as to our bet would have to go over to the next term.

After starting for home, while running down the bog, Mr. Sawyer killed three noble black ducks at one shot, but the gun was not loaded this time with ball. Mr. Hanson struck with his fishing-pole

*Water-
snakes*

and killed a monstrous water-snake. Mr. Little measured a stick with his hands, and, using it as a rule, declared him to be five feet long. If I thought any such snakes ever went over to Dingley Bay, I never would go into the water there again.

When we got out of the bog into the open water, we found a lively breeze from the northwest, and they landed me at the Dingley Brook in less than an hour, and then kept on like a great white bird down towards the Cape and for the outlet. I stood and watched the boat till it was nearly halfway to Frye's Island, loath to lose sight of what had helped me to enjoy the day so much.

*A string
of worth-
less fish*

Taking my fish, I walked home, and greeted mother just as the sun went out of sight behind the hills of Baldwin. The fish were worthless, and it made me sweat to carry them; but I thought I must have something to show for the day spent. After exhibiting them to

mother and sister, and hearing the com-
ments as to their ugliness, and much spec-
ulation as to what their horns were for, I
gave them to Mr. Lambard, who said
pouts were the best of all fish after they
were skinned.

I have made this account of the expe- *Written*
dition to please uncle Richard, who is *for uncle*
an invalid, and cannot get out to enjoy *Richard*
such sport, and wished me to write and
describe everything just as it happened,
whether witty or silly, and give my own
impressions. He has read my diary, and
says it interested him, which is all the
reward I desire. And now I add these
lines to keep in remembrance the peculiar satisfaction I received in hearing the
conversation, particularly of Mr. Deblois
and Mr. Little.

RAYMOND, August, 1818.

[There were curious facts not known
to Hawthorne which give peculiar interest to some particulars in the above

97

sketch. The present writer had some personal acquaintance in later years with both Thomas Amory Deblois and Matthias Plant Sawyer, and knows a good reason why the men laughed at the sally about "turning the fish into a pack of cards," — a joke of which Hawthorne could not see the point. "Plant" Sawyer, as he was always called, was a rich bachelor, who was said to have acquired much of his wealth as "a votary of chance," to use his own expression. He had drawn large prizes in lotteries, and was reputed a most skillful card-player. He might well say that "chance had treated him handsomely." In the manipulation of cards he had the skill of a professional juggler ; and a similar dexterity no doubt he displayed in puzzling the boys by changing the fish from one string to the other. The men in the party knew of his skill with cards, and of course understood and laughed at the allusion made by Deblois. About twenty years after the expedition so graphically described by Hawthorne, Mr. Sawyer, then an old man, removed to Boston, and became a State Street broker. He owned and occupied the mansion at the corner of Beacon and Park streets. Deblois was afterward a partner in the law firm of Fessenden, Deblois and Fessenden, the junior partner of which was the statesman, William Pitt Fessenden. As to the jews'-harp man, the late Hon. William Goold informed me that he was a blacksmith named Goodrich, who made clumsy harps at his forge. If the harps the Jews hung on the willows were as large as his, Goold thought "one to a willow was sufficient!" In reference to the invalidism of "uncle Richard," it may be said that Mr. Manning had been disabled by a carriage accident, and was for a long time obliged to get about his house in a wheel-chair.]   .

Story of
William
Symmes

SHORTLY after the death of Symmes the following notice of him appeared in the Georgetown (D. C.) " Courier." It is full of curious information, and suggests reasons for the mystery he observed in communicating the extracts from the diary he claimed to have in his possession. I am informed that the names of persons and places he assumed as aliases in his detective work are all recognized at Otisfield as *real* men and localities he must have been familiar with in his youth. In our search for the diary an appeal was made to the government detectives, and perhaps this was checkmated by him by means of his familiarity with that department, of which we then knew nothing. The obituary notice is here given in full, as it may help in the finding of the long-lost book. It was published early in November, 1871 : —

"Died at Pensacola, Florida, on the *Obituary* 28th ultimo, William Symmes, aged sixty- *notice* six years. He was a mulatto, born in Portland, Maine, his father having been a white man and a lawyer, the late William Symmes; his mother a pure African. His father was in early life a tutor in Virginia, and was never married. When three years old the son was adopted by the late Captain Jonathan Britton, of Otisfield, Cumberland County, Maine, and by him given a good common school education. At the age of twenty-one he became a sailor, following the sea for twenty-five years, and visiting every part of the globe. In 1852 he drifted into California, remaining there eight years, and getting acquainted with the late Colonel Lafayette C. Baker, and was with him, under half a dozen names, in and about the District of Columbia during the war. Soldiers and others will remember the darky who used to hang around Baker's office, and call him-

self at different times by the following
names : 'Asa Hicks,' 'Thad. Turner,'
'Caswell's Corner,' 'Deacon Lovell,' 'College Swamp,' 'Deacon Hancock,' etc.
He kept a journal during his connection
with Baker, which will perhaps be a curiosity.   His foster father, Captain Britton, was intimate with the late General
Samuel Fessenden, father of the late
senator, and also with the family of the
Two late Nathaniel Hawthorne ; and Symmes
famous used to play with William Pitt Fessen-
playmates den and Nathaniel Hawthorne when they
were striplings.   He boasted within a
few years that he was the only man at
the seat of government with whom Senator Fessenden would laugh and joke
familiarly ; and that he and Hawthorne
were the only two white boys and men
who never by word or look offended him
in the matter of his color.   Symmes did
not belong to the regular force of detectives, but Baker kept him as a kind of
detective on his own men.   The last two

years of his life he became a devoted Methodist, and would repeat by the half hour hymns from the old 'Bridgewater Collection,' that he said his foster mother, Beulah Britton, taught him in his youth. He was also a constant reader of the Bible. Poor Symmes has gone. Since the war he has lived secluded in Alexandria and Georgetown, not daring to face openly the enemies he made under Baker. May he rest in peace."

Of his life as a boy at Otisfield, Robinson Cook says : " Billy was reared in this neighborhood, from the age of three to twenty years, and was a boy of fair intellect. He attended school at the old *Symmes* schoolhouse near the parsonage, but was *at school* too full of his joking to make any remarkable proficiency in his studies. When he had done going to school he could write a fair hand, and read and spell tolerably well."

The fact that General Fessenden was an acquaintance of Captain Britton may

account for the adoption of young
Symmes; for Fessenden came to the
Cumberland bar before the death of the
older Symmes, and may have taken an
interest in the orphaned mulatto boy.
His own son, William Pitt, was one year
younger than Symmes, and as they grew
up, they had many opportunities of playing together. Not only did young Fessenden often visit the Sebago Lake region, but Captain Britton represented his
town in the Maine legislature, which
then held its sessions at Portland, the
home of the Fessendens.

*His an-
cestry*   Zechariah Symmes, the first of the
American ancestors of the subject of this
sketch, was son and grandson of clergymen who suffered in the Marian perse-
cution. He was born in Canterbury, in
1599, and his father was Rev. William
Symmes, who was ordained in 1588. He
was first a lecturer at Atholines, London,
but, being harassed for nonconformity,
removed to Dunstable in 1625. In 1634

he came to this country in the same ship which brought the noted Anne Hutchinson. He became pastor of the first church in Charlestown, Massachusetts, and had for assistant no less a personage than John Harvard, the founder of the college which has immortalized his name. He died in 1671, and for epitaph has this couplet : —

> " A prophet lies under this stone :
> His words shall live, though he be gone."

His son, Zechariah, was a graduate of *A race of* Harvard, class of 1657, the first scholar *clergymen* of his class, and was a tutor in the college for three years. He became first pastor of the church in Bradford in 1667, and died in 1707. He is spoken of as a man of rare ability and great physical endurance, as he could preach and pray four or five hours before an audience of equal "staying power." He was followed in the Bradford pastorate by his son, Thomas, who also graduated at Harvard at the head of his class, in 1698, and

105

was tutor for three years. He preached the "election sermon" at the Old South in 1720. It is said of him that in preaching he magnified his office, "lifting up his voice like a trumpet, and preaching with all his might." He raised a mutiny in his church by insisting that the singing should be by *note* and in *parts*, and carried his point. The objection was that the Papists sang by note, but this and other objections he riddled with satire. The excitement ran so high, we are told, that women fainted away when singing by note was first heard in the meeting-house. He died in 1725. The next Harvard graduates in the family were Timothy, 1733, William, 1750, and William, Jr., 1780, — this last being the Portland lawyer, whose ancestors, for six generations, were Puritan clergymen. It must be allowed that our colored friend, William Symmes, fourth of the name, the playmate of Hawthorne, came of good stock, and there is no occasion to wonder that with little schooling he attained the literary skill shown in the letters of his given in this volume. For three centuries his ancestors of the name of Symmes were all college graduates.

RICHARD MANNING, of Salem, *The* the father of Mrs. Hawthorne, *Manning* toward the close of the last century, ac- *estate in Maine* quired possession of several thousands of acres of land in Cumberland County, Maine, mostly in what are now the towns of Raymond and Casco. He also owned land in Bridgeton, Westbrook, and Portland. At his death this land was not divided among his family, but in 1813 his son Robert was made attorney of the heirs for the management of the estate. His brother Richard became a resident of Raymond and married Susan Dingley, a daughter of Captain Samuel Dingley, the miller mentioned in the Hawthorne notes, who was a son of the first settler in the town.   The management of the Manning lands was then given to Richard, who acted as attorney for all the heirs, until about 1830.   He died in 1831, aged forty-seven years.

I find by reference to the records in the registry of deeds in Portland that between the years of 1813 and 1840, about twelve thousand acres of land were sold to settlers, in lots averaging one hundred acres each.   All the deeds given *Deeds signed by Mrs. Hathorne* between the dates mentioned were signed by Elizabeth C. Hathorne, as one of the heirs.   In all cases her name is spelled without the "w."   In the deeds given in 1820 and 1821, she is described as a resident of Raymond.   In earlier deeds she is made a resident of Salem, even in 1818, when all the biographies place her in Raymond.   Probably her residence in the Maine wilderness was not considered permanent until 1820.

The other heirs of the estate, as shown in the deeds, were Miriam, Mrs. Hawthorne's mother, who lived until 1831 ; Mary and Priscilla, her sisters, described as "single women," until Priscilla became the wife of John Dike; Robert and Samuel, her brothers, "stage proprietors;" and Richard Manning, "trader," of Raymond. Nearly all the names mentioned by Hawthorne in his first notebook are found in these deeds. Dominicus Jordan, the peddler, who told the ghost story, pp. 77–79, bought no less than seven hundred acres of the estate at various times. His wife was Kezia Dingley, a relative of Hawthorne's aunt, Susan Manning. The father of unfortunate Henry Jackson, Jr., who was put "out of the reach of mercy" by having his mouth kicked open (see pp. 61, 62), bought one hundred acres of land of the Manning estate in 1808. The good Elder Zachariah Leach, who had such dread forebodings as to the future of Jackson, was also a purchaser of these lands.

The Manning brothers owned an important line of Eastern stages, and the horses of this line were at the service of Hawthorne in his journeyings back and forth between Salem and his Maine home.

Served in war of 1812

WASHINGTON LONGLEY, mentioned by Hawthorne on page 56, was an expert drummer and a teacher of the art, at the time when he came to the grist-mill. He served as drummer in a company, enlisted at Waterford, Maine, in the war of 1812. After the war he settled at Raymond, on a lot purchased of the Mannings on the shore of Panther Pond. This was in the year 1817, which is the probable date of the entry in the note-book. His son, who now lives in the house built by his father, informs me that he remembers the colored man, William Symmes, who called at his father's house in 1840. He has a more distinct memory of him because, as a boy who had never before seen a black man, he was frightened. His mother lived in the family of Captain Jonathan Britton at the time when Symmes had a home there, and the sailor came to talk of old times. He is described as a man of average height, strongly built, and of dark color for a mulatto.

The only person I find in Raymond who remembers Hawthorne is Hezekiah Lombard, who was born in 1816, and was six years old when Mrs. Hawthorne gave up her residence in the town. He says she returned to Salem in January, 1822. He also remembers Symmes, who was in the vicinity for some years after the Hawthornes left.

One living who remembers

111

INDEX

113

INDEX

114

INDEX

www.ingramcontent.com/pod-product-compliance
Lightning Source LLC
Chambersburg PA
CBHW020410030726
47496CB00007B/2387